Eerie Elementary

Sam
BATTLES
the
Machine!

By Jack Chabert
Illustrated by Sam Ricks

BRANCHES

SCHOLASTIC INC.

READ ALL THE
Eerie Elementary
ADVENTURES!

MORE BOOKS
COMING SOON!

Table of Contents

To teachers and librarians everywhere – thank you! — JC

Text copyright © 2017 by Max Brallier
Illustrations copyright © 2017 Scholastic Inc.

Chabert, Jack, author.
Sam BATTLES the Machine! / by Jack Chabert; illustrated by Sam Ricks.—First edition.
pages cm.—(Eerie Elementary ; 6)
Summary: Sam, Lucy, and Antonio have a new substitute teacher, who happens to be the great-great-grandson of Orson Eerie, the evil scientist whose spirit possesses and infects their elementary school—and the friends are afraid he may be trying to bring Orson back to life.
ISBN 978-0-545-87378-9 (pbk. :alk. paper)—ISBN 978-0-545-87379-6 (hardcover :alk.paper)
1. Substitute teachers—Juvenile fiction. 2. Haunted schools—Juvenile fiction.
3. Scientists—Juvenile fiction. 4. Inheritance and succession—Juvenile fiction.
5. Elementary schools—Juvenile fiction. 6. Best friends—Juvenile fiction.
[1. Substitute teachers—Fiction. 2. Haunted places—Fiction. 3. Scientists—Fiction.
4. Schools—Fiction. 5. Best friends—Fiction. 6. Friendship—Fiction.]
Ricks, Sam, illustrator. II. Title. III. Series: Chabert, Jack. Eerie Elementary ; 6.
LCC PZ7.C3313 Or 2017
813.6—dc23 LC [Fic]
2016045590

ISBN 978-0-545-87379-6 (hardcover) / ISBN 978-0-545-87378-9 (paperback)

10 9 8 7 6 5 4 3   19 20 21 22 23

Printed in China   62

First edition, May 2017
Illustrated by Sam Ricks
Edited by Katie Carella
Book design by Maria Mercado

STRANGE NEW SUBSTITUTE

"Where's Ms. Grinker?" Sam Graves asked. It was Monday morning, and he was walking into his third grade classroom with his best friends, Antonio and Lucy.

"Are you serious, Sam?" Antonio asked. "How could you forget? I've been looking forward to this!"

"Looking forward to what?" Sam asked.

"We have a substitute teacher *all week!*" Lucy exclaimed. "Ms. Grinker is on vacation, remember?"

Sam had *completely* forgotten. As he took his seat, he felt the extreme happiness that only comes with . . . a substitute teacher! Everyone knows a week with a substitute teacher is *the best week.*

"I bet we won't have, like, any classwork!" Antonio said.

Sam smiled. A week without schoolwork would be relaxing — and Sam and his friends were in serious need of a relaxing week . . .

Mr. Nekobi, the man who took care of the school, had chosen Sam to be the school's hall monitor. He had told Sam the truth about Eerie Elementary: It was alive! It was a living, breathing thing! A monster! And this was a secret that Mr. Nekobi had only shared with Sam, Antonio, and Lucy. Nothing about *school* had been relaxing since Mr. Nekobi told them the truth.

"Who do you think our sub will be?" Sam asked his friends.

Lucy pointed. "It looks like we're about to find out."

The school principal, Mr. Winik, appeared in the doorway. Principal Winik was tall and sturdy. He wore thick black glasses. "Class," the principal said, "as you know, you have a substitute teacher this week. Please treat him  with the same respect you would Ms. Grinker."

Mr. Winik left, and the substitute teacher rushed into the room. The substitute moved in short, quick spurts. He was tall, but he was so bone-thin that he almost seemed *see-through*.

Sam thought the man looked familiar, but he wasn't sure *why*.

The substitute teacher hurried to the white-board, nearly tripping over a chair. Someone giggled. Then he began writing his name on the board.

Lucy nudged Sam. "What's he wearing?"

"He's dressed like my great-grandpa!" Antonio said, chuckling quietly.

But an instant later, Lucy and Antonio stopped laughing. The teacher had finished writing and turned to face the classroom.

Sam read the name on the board. It sent a cold chill down his spine. His hands began to tremble, and he felt light-headed. He was *terrified*.

The new substitute teacher's name was:

Mr. Eerie

ANOTHER EERIE?!

Sam's heart was beating like a drum. He read the name on the board over and over. Each time, he hoped it would be different.

But no. The substitute teacher's name was Mr. Eerie.

Could this guy be related to Orson Eerie? Sam wondered.

Orson Eerie was the architect who designed Eerie Elementary almost one hundred years ago. He was also a mad scientist. Orson Eerie found a way to live forever — he became the school. Eerie Elementary was Orson Eerie.

Sam and his friends had battled Eerie Elementary many times. A few weeks earlier, they made a bone-chilling discovery: Orson Eerie was trying to come back to life — *as a real, flesh-and-blood person!*

Sam's mind was racing. *Could this guy* be *Orson Eerie? Did he actually come back to life?*

Sam turned to Antonio and Lucy. He saw fear splashed across their faces.

CLAP!

Mr. Eerie clapped. The entire class sat up, at attention.

"Class," the substitute said, "please open your science books to Chapter Eight: Basic Tools and Building — "

"Argh, can't we just watch a movie today?" one student asked.

"Or have silent drawing time?" another student asked.

"Open your books," Mr. Eerie repeated.

Sam glanced at his friends as he opened his textbook. They needed to talk, but couldn't! Sam tried to pay attention, but that name kept running through his head: *Mr. Eerie, Mr. Eerie, Mr. Eerie . . .*

RIIIIING!

Finally, the lunch bell rang. Mr. Eerie was the first to leave. He scooped up his bag and rushed out of the classroom. He nearly knocked over two chairs and one student!

"It's *really* good that all three of us have hall monitor duty now," Sam said as he followed Antonio and Lucy into the hall. "So we can talk about this weirdness before we're at lunch with everyone else!"

The three friends whispered as they walked the halls.

"This new substitute looks *so much like* Orson Eerie," Sam said. "As soon as I saw him, I got the creeps."

"Let's not freak out yet," Lucy replied. "He is probably a relative of Orson's. Like his great-great-nephew or something."

"You're right," Sam agreed.

Antonio threw up his hands. "Were you guys born yesterday?!" he exclaimed. "Our substitute teacher is a ZOMBIE! *Orson Eerie came back to life as a zombie!*"

Lucy and Sam stopped in their tracks.

Could Antonio be right?

Sam wondered.

BIZARRE BEHAVIOR...

3

"Zombie Orson Eerie? Really?" Lucy asked. "Don't be ridiculous, Antonio. Zombies aren't real!"

"I did not think monstrous, living schools were real, either," Antonio shot back. "But they are!"

Sam shook his head. "Lucy's right. Our new substitute teacher might be weird — but he's not a *zombie*."

Just then, Sam spotted Mr. Eerie far down the hall. Mr. Eerie glanced around, like he was making sure no one was watching.

Sam yanked Lucy and Antonio behind the water fountain.

"What are you doing?" Lucy exclaimed.

"Look!" Sam said. "Mr. Eerie is up to something sneaky!"

But when they turned to look, Mr. Eerie was gone!

Something was wrong. Sam *felt* it. He had a twisted and tangled feeling in his gut. As hall monitor, Sam could sense things that other students couldn't. He could *feel* when something was wrong. And right now, Sam had that feeling.

RiNG! It was the final lunch bell. Students hurried toward the lunchroom.

Sam leapt up and ran down the hall.

"Where are you going?" Lucy called out.

"Just cover for me at lunch!" Sam shouted.

Antonio called after Sam, but Sam just kept running.

Sam followed Mr. Eerie all the way to an empty hall at the far end of the school.

Sam watched. The teacher seemed to be carefully examining the school. He felt the walls. He knocked on pipes. He leaned close to the lockers. His mouth moved, like he was whispering.

What's he doing? Sam wondered.

Suddenly, at the end of the hall —
CREEAAAK! The music room door slowly
swung open.

Who opened that door? It's lunchtime, Sam
thought. *The music room should be empty.*

Mr. Eerie stepped through the doorway.
The door slammed shut behind him.

The twisted and tangled feeling in Sam's
stomach grew. Something awful was about to
happen!

Sam raced toward the room . . .

MUSIC ROOM MYSTERY

Sam slid to a stop at the music room door. He peered through the window.

Mr. Eerie was standing in the center of the room. He appeared to be speaking. But there was no one there.

Is he talking to Orson? Sam thought. He couldn't hear through the door.

Next, Mr. Eerie's eyes shot down to the floor. Something was happening . . .

The shaggy carpet threads started rising and twisting. Sam gasped. In moments, they grew as tall as overgrown grass! They quickly wrapped around both of Mr. Eerie's ankles like tentacles.

Sam saw panic on Mr. Eerie's face — he was trapped!

I have to do something! Sam thought. *I don't know much about Mr. Eerie — but I* do *know how powerful Eerie Elementary is!*

Sam threw open the door and burst inside.

The teacher whirled around. "What are you — " He wasn't able to finish his sentence. The carpet-tentacles circled Mr. Eerie's wrists and tugged —

CRASH! He fell face-first to the floor.

BA-RRANG! The classroom's grand piano suddenly jerked and jumped! The black-and-white keys looked like teeth. The piano opened, then snapped shut like a monstrous musical mouth.

Oh no! thought Sam. *The carpet-tentacles are dragging Mr. Eerie toward that monster! He'll be piano chow!*

Sam's eyes darted across the room. He spotted a recorder on the music teacher's desk and scooped it up. "I'm coming!" he shouted.

Mr. Eerie cried out as the carpet-tentacles pulled him toward the piano. Sam raced forward, swinging the recorder like a sword.

With each swing, Sam sliced through more of the strange carpet-tentacles. At last, he freed Mr. Eerie!

The piano keys banged, clanged, and then went silent.

VOOSH!

Something brushed against Sam's ankle. One carpet thread remained. It slithered like a ferocious snake.

It snapped out, but Sam jumped up and *squashed* it. "Gotcha!" he said.

Finally, the room was still.

Mr. Eerie stared open-mouthed at Sam. "Can . . . ? Could . . . ?"

He's in shock, Sam realized. "Are you okay?" he asked.

Mr. Eerie didn't answer.

"Who *are* you, really?" Sam asked. "Why are you *here*?"

Mr. Eerie simply scrambled to his feet and raced away.

Now Sam knew one thing for certain: Mr. Eerie was *somehow* involved with the monstrous school. The school had revealed its powers to him. That was *new*. Aside from Mr. Nekobi, Lucy, Antonio, and Sam himself, no one else knew about the scary adventures that occurred within the walls of Eerie Elementary.

RING!

Recess. It was time to tell Antonio and Lucy that something *very strange* was going on with their substitute teacher.

Sam rushed outside to the playground.

A STUNNING DISCOVERY

5

He spotted Lucy and Antonio on the swing set. Lucy was looking in an open book.

"We've been doing research!" Lucy said as Sam ran over.

Antonio tossed an apple to Sam. "Thought you might be hungry after missing lunch," he said.

Sam smiled and took a chomp. Then he looked down at the book in Lucy's hands, *Eerie: A Town History.* He saw the Eerie family tree. At the bottom was a photo of a young boy. The boy's name was Jasper Eerie.

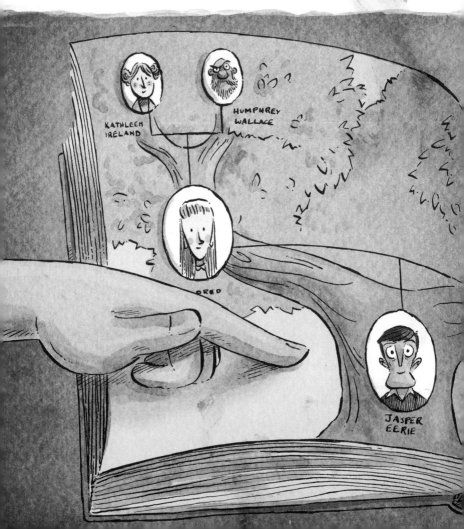

"That's our substitute!" Lucy said, poking the page. "He just looks younger because this book is so old."

Sam studied the page. "Unbelievable. This means our substitute is Orson Eerie's great-great-grandson."

Antonio crossed his arms. "I'm not buying it. I still think he's Zombie Orson."

"He's not Zombie Orson!" Lucy said. "And why does it seem like you *want* a Zombie Orson?"

Antonio shrugged. "Zombies are cool."

"Guys, listen," Sam said. "I have to tell you what just happened!"

Antonio and Lucy moved closer to Sam. "I followed Mr. Eerie — *Jasper* — to the music room," Sam said. "And he got *attacked* by the school!"

"If the school attacked him, that means he's not bad, right?" Lucy asked.

"He's *definitely* bad," Antonio replied. "His last name is Eerie!"

"I'm not sure if he's good or bad," Sam said. "Maybe Orson was battling Jasper like he battles us — to take him down. But . . . remember Orson Eerie's science book? It said Orson wanted to come back to life — *for real*. Maybe Jasper's helping Orson, but Orson just got mad at him for some reason."

"The only way to find out," Lucy said, "is to learn more about Jasper."

Sam narrowed his eyes. He leaned close and said, "After school, we'll follow Jasper Eerie. We'll see where he goes. And we'll find out what he's up to."

THE CHASE!

6

$\mathbf{S}$am was relieved when the day was over. Ever since lunch, he had been jumpy — and so had Jasper Eerie. The substitute teacher was clearly flustered. He simply told the students to read quietly. But Sam hadn't been able to concentrate. And every time he looked up from his book, Jasper Eerie was watching him.

Students and teachers headed home.

But Sam, Antonio, and Lucy headed to the playground.

They all hid behind the jungle gym, watching the exit. They were waiting for Jasper to leave.

"There he is!" Sam whispered.

"Look!" Lucy said. "Jasper is carrying one of Orson's creepy old journals. It looks like the one we found in the school basement after the locker swallowed me up."

Antonio gulped. "That is not a good sign . . ."

Jasper unlocked a rusty bicycle from the bike rack. He glanced around, like he knew he was being watched.

Then he sped away.

"Come on!" Sam said.

The friends ran after him.

"Careful!" Lucy added. "We can't let him see us!"

When Jasper stopped at a crosswalk, the friends ducked behind an oak tree. Peeking around it, Antonio said, "I feel like I'm in a spy movie!"

Lucy smiled. "That's better than most days. Usually, it feels like we're in a *horror* movie!"

Jasper rode faster. Sam and his friends had to sprint to keep up.

Soon, Jasper turned down a shadowy street. The friends heard his bicycle rattle to a halt.

Sam's side was hurting as he sped around the corner. He glanced both ways down the sidewalk, but there was no sign of their substitute teacher.

"He disappeared!" Antonio exclaimed.

"He must've known we were on to him," Lucy said, kicking the ground.

Sam eyed the old, tall houses that lined the crooked street. Then he spotted it.

"Look!" Sam said, pointing to a rusted iron fence.

Jasper's bicycle sat at the end of a cracked driveway that led to a rundown house. The house's windows were broken, and the roof was sunken in. Dead weeds covered the lawn.

If Eerie Elementary were a house, this is what it would look like, thought Sam.

"That house was in the library book!" Lucy exclaimed. She pulled *Eerie: A Town History* from her backpack. Her face lit up as she flipped through the pages. "This was Orson Eerie's house. This is where he lived

Sam couldn't believe it: He was staring at the home of his enemy. *Just imagine how many secrets this house must hold*, he thought.

For a long moment, the friends didn't say anything. They were too terrified to speak.

Lucy shut the book.

"We need to find out why *Jasper* is living in this house," Antonio said.

Sam stepped toward the iron fence. "We need to get inside. Now."

THE HOUSE OF ORSON EERIE

7

"I can't believe we're doing this," Antonio whispered. "We're going into the house of *Zombie Orson Eerie* . . ."

"Antonio, now we know Jasper is *not* a zombie!" Lucy said. "He's just Orson Eerie's great-great-grandson!"

"His *zombie* grandson," Antonio muttered.

The friends climbed over the fence.

Glancing up at the house, Sam saw that the windows were all dark.

"This way," Sam whispered.

The back door of the house was red, but the paint was chipping. Sam gently took hold of the door handle. He began to turn the knob, but it came off in his hand. It was like the door had rotted away to nothing. Sam swallowed and pushed the door open.

Antonio pinched his nose. "This house smells like a damp basement."

Sam glanced back at his friends. He could tell they didn't want to go any farther. He didn't either. But they *had* to learn the truth.

Slowly, Sam tiptoed inside. His friends followed.

Darkness filled the big house. It felt like something horrible might leap from the shadows at any moment. An old radio hissed soft static.

The friends crept ahead. A large, curved staircase led upstairs. Lucy opened her mouth to speak, but —

BOOM! BOOM! BA-BLAM!

"Something just exploded!" Antonio said.

"It came from upstairs!" Lucy added.

Sam's eyes darted to the top of the staircase.

"Come on!"

CAUGHT!

8

BOOM!   BOOM!
BA-BLAM!

There was another series of booms. Bright flashing lights came from the second floor.

Sam grabbed the railing, trying to calm his nerves. The steps creaked and groaned. His heart pounded as he climbed to the top.

The friends peered into the first room on the right. It was pitch black. They couldn't see a thing. But then a bright flash of light lit it up for a moment.

Sam choked back a gasp. He saw that there was a large, strange machine in the room. Jasper Eerie stood before it. His hair was wild, like that of a mad scientist.

Antonio ducked back into the hall. "Okay, I was wrong. Jasper is not a zombie. It's worse!" he said to Sam and Lucy. "He's like *Dr. Frankenstein*! He's bringing Orson back to life. Right here! Right now!"

"That sounds *nuts*," Sam said. "But it could be true . . ."

Sam took a step back, but as he did — he bumped into Lucy.

"Oof!" Lucy exclaimed. Her foot slipped on the top step. Her eyes went wide as she began falling backward.

Antonio caught her just before she tumbled down the staircase.

"Sorry, Lucy," Sam whispered.

As he turned to look back into the room, he almost screamed.

Jasper had heard them! His eyes were locked with Sam's.

"Run!" Sam shouted.

The three friends dashed down the hall. But as they ran into another room, a shadow flashed ahead of them. Jasper had somehow made it into the room first.

There must be shortcuts hidden inside this house, Sam thought.

The tall man was now blocking their way.
"You kids shouldn't be here," Jasper Eerie
growled as he stomped toward them . . .

THE MYSTERIOUS MACHINE

"What are you doing in my house?" Jasper Eerie demanded. He loomed over Sam, Lucy, and Antonio.

The friends were cornered!

Sam swallowed and stepped forward. "We know the truth about the school and about Orson Eerie," he said. "And *I* know you know what I'm talking about. We were both there, in the music room . . ."

Jasper's eyes widened as he looked to Antonio and Lucy. "All *three* of you know the school is alive?"

Antonio nodded. *"And* we know you're trying to bring Orson back to life!"

"But we won't let you!" Lucy said, balling up her fists.

Relief swept across Jasper's face. "Bring Orson back to life?" he said. "Oh, no! It's the opposite."

Sam looked to Lucy and Antonio. Their mouths were small, stern lines.

"I apologize if I scared you," Jasper said, speaking softly. "But if you follow me, I can show you *the real truth* about Orson and your school."

Sam and his friends couldn't resist the opportunity to learn more. They followed their substitute teacher.

"Orson Eerie and I are related. Orson was my great-great-grandfather. This old house is mine — I inherited it," Jasper said. "After moving in, I discovered a trunk *full* of Orson's notebooks and designs. He wrote about *your elementary school*. And I found plans for the strange machine that allowed Orson to *become* the school . . ."

"A machine?" Lucy asked.

Jasper nodded. "I didn't think it was real. But I was curious. So when Principal Winik posted for a substitute teacher, I applied. It was the only way I could investigate the school and learn if Orson had been successful. Today, I did something I *thought* was crazy: I spoke to the school. But it wasn't crazy . . . The school heard me — *Orson Eerie* heard me! And attacked me! That's when I knew it was true. All of it . . ."

Jasper led the three friends inside the shadowy room.

It took a minute for Sam's eyes to adjust to the darkness. Then he fully saw the strange machine. It was the size of a refrigerator. It was built from many different parts, all of which appeared to be very old. Sam saw an ancient stove, a boxy TV, vacuum hoses, and other things.

"*Orson* built this?" Antonio asked.

"Sort of," Jasper said. "I found it here. It was a wreck. I started to rebuild it. I believe I can use this machine to do the *opposite* of what Orson did. I believe it can *remove* Orson from the school — so that the two are no longer bound together."

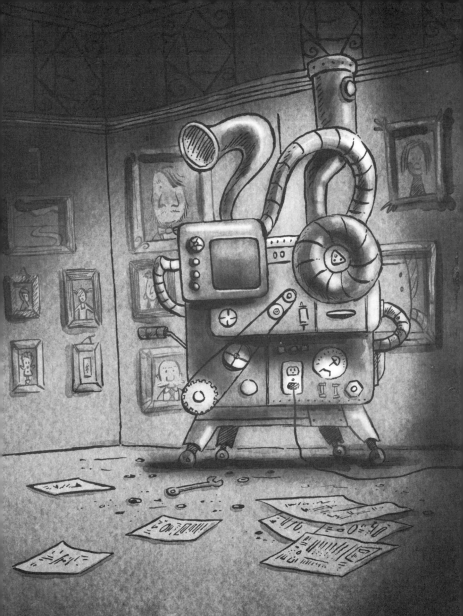

"Wait," Sam said. "You mean, this machine

"I hope . . ." Jasper said with a heavy sigh. He sat down. "But what happened at the school today . . . It terrified me. I hurried home today, planning to destroy the machine."

"You can't do that!" Lucy exclaimed. "It might be what we need to defeat Eerie Elementary once and for all!"

Sam stepped forward. "Mr. Eerie! Please! You might be the only one who can help us."

Jasper looked worn out, but he managed a nod. "Okay," he said. "But the machine is not yet complete . . ."

Sam rolled up his sleeves. "Then let's get to work."

A PLAN COMES TOGETHER

Jasper Eerie led Sam, Lucy, and Antonio over to a desk. There were towering stacks of faded, crinkly papers. They contained sketches and scribbles.

"These papers hold Orson's plans for the machine," Mr. Eerie explained. "We need to go through them and *reverse* his directions. We need to make the machine work *backward*. And I'll need your help."

Sam and Lucy picked up tools.

Antonio eyed the desk. "I'm good at cursive, so I'll read the plans to you three," Antonio said, grabbing some papers. He sat cross-legged on the floor.

With that, they got to work . . .

"Switch the vacuum cleaner to reverse mode," Antonio called out.

Sam unbolted, removed, and reattached parts.

Lucy slid underneath the huge machine. "Screwdriver!" she said. Jasper handed it to her. Next, she called out, "Pliers!" and he rushed them over.

When Lucy slid out from beneath the machine, she was covered in grease and soot.

"It's like putting together a Lego set," Lucy said, smiling.

"And we're making progress," said Jasper, turning a knob.

Finally, Antonio pointed to a large red lever atop the machine. "There's only one last thing to do," he said. "Turn it on . . ."

Sam climbed on to the machine. He held his breath as he pulled the lever.

VROOOOOOOM! A loud, high-pitched roar filled the room. The machine rumbled and smoked!

Sam hung on as it shook faster and howled louder.

"The whole neighborhood will hear that!" Mr. Eerie exclaimed. "Turn it off!"

Just as Sam yanked the lever to OFF, he was flung across the room.

The machine went still.

Jasper helped Sam to his feet. With a smile, he said, "I believe we've done it. Good work, students."

Antonio set down the papers. Lucy grabbed a rag and cleaned her hands. Sam wiped soot from his nose.

"Tomorrow," Sam said. "We remove Orson Eerie from Eerie Elementary — once and for all . . ."

CLOSE CALL!

The next day, Sam, Lucy, and Antonio arrived at school early. Mr. Eerie was waiting with the machine. It was hidden beneath a tattered orange-and-green quilt.

Working together, they lifted the machine up the steps and into the school. The wheels squeaked as they pushed it down the hall.

"Phew," Lucy said. "I'm glad we got this thing inside before anyone else arrived."

"Yeah," Antonio agreed. "Imagine trying to explain what's underneath this quilt!"

But just as Antonio said that, he stepped on a corner of the quilt. **WHOOSH!** The quilt was yanked off the machine.

At that exact moment, Principal Winik stepped from his office.

Oh no! Sam thought. *Of course the principal is here early. Our timing couldn't be any worse!*

It took Principal Winik about two seconds to notice the machine and about another two seconds for his face to scrunch up. "What exactly is going on here?"

Mr. Eerie appeared speechless. Sam had no clue what to say, either. But then —

"They're assisting me!" a voice said.

Sam spun around. Relief flooded through him. It was Mr. Nekobi.

"Mr. Winik, this is a heavy-duty cleaning machine," Mr. Nekobi explained. "I asked the hall monitors to help me bring it into school early — and Mr. Eerie is helping. I'll be using it to scrub the paint-stained floors in the art room."

Principal Winik's face lit up. "Just in time for parent-teacher visits! Carry on."

Mr. Nekobi helped Jasper Eerie, Antonio, Lucy, and Sam push the machine toward the art room.

"I better figure out a way to clean those floors now," Mr. Nekobi whispered to Sam with a chuckle.

Sam laughed, but only for a moment. "Mr. Nekobi!" Sam exclaimed. "I have to tell you everything we've learned! Mr. Eerie is related to Orson Eerie, and this machine —"

Mr. Nekobi interrupted Sam. "No need," he said. "I will always be here to cover for you and to tell you what I know. But my days of fighting the school are over."

Sam nodded. "I understand."

Mr. Nekobi turned away, leaving them to their mission.

Soon they had pushed the machine into the art room. They hid it behind paint cans and boxes of erasers.

"Okay," Sam said, "Let's meet here right after the final bell."

Jasper ran a shaky hand through his hair. Antonio slapped him on the shoulder. "Don't worry, Mr. Eerie! We're used to these sorts of adventures!"

Sam looked at the machine one last time before Jasper covered it with the quilt. *I hope this works.*

He turned to his friends and saw confident grins on their faces. For the first time, they felt hopeful about really beating Eerie Elementary.

Sam didn't want to disappoint them. That's why he didn't mention the feeling in the pit of his stomach. And that's why he didn't mention the feeling that everything was going to go horribly wrong . . .

POWERING UP

12

When the final bell rang, Sam and his friends sprinted to the art room.

"Ready?" Jasper Eerie asked, greeting them. He was wheeling the huge machine out from its hiding place.

"You bet!" Antonio said. He and Lucy helped Sam clear away chairs and tables, creating space.

The machine looked enormous as Jasper pushed it into the center of the room. He plugged in the power cord.

"Run the hoses to the walls," Jasper said, reading from Orson's old notes. "We need the machine to be as *connected* to the school as possible."

Antonio attached hoses to air ducts. Sam and Lucy shoved tubes against cracks in the cinder-block wall.

Then they all stared at the machine.

Sam thought he saw something odd. He stepped closer. He couldn't quite tell. But it looked like — ever so slowly — a single screw was turning. *Oh no. Orson Eerie knows what we're doing!*

"We can't wait any longer," Sam said. He stepped up onto a chair, grabbed hold of the machine's red lever, and pulled.

BRRRR-ROOOOM! Sam jumped down as the machine rumbled to life.

"Um, so what's supposed to happen now?" Antonio asked.

The machine chugged and pumped. The hoses shook and snapped against the floor.

"Just give it time . . ." Lucy replied.

All of a sudden, Lucy's hair stood on end. Sam felt his own hair do the same. "The machine is creating static electricity," Lucy said. "Like when you rub your feet on the carpet and then touch a door knob."

The air in the room felt electric. A strange wind began to blow. Papers whirled around. The curtains waved and the lights flickered.

Suddenly, the color of the walls seemed to lighten — from top to bottom. It was like the darkness of Orson Eerie was being drained from the school.

"It's working!" Jasper shouted over the rumbling machine.

But Sam wasn't so sure. The bad feeling in his stomach was growing stronger. Then —

The ceiling lights **BURST!** Sam, Lucy, and Antonio reeled back as the floor buckled. The room turned pitch black. Jasper tripped.

Everything was quiet. No one dared speak. No one dared even breathe.

Then it happened.

For the first time, Sam and his friends heard the voice of Orson Eerie. Orson Eerie *spoke* to them. And what he said chilled them to their bones . . .

HE SPEAKS AT LAST!

Orson Eerie's voice echoed off the gray cinder-block walls. **"FOOLS! YOU CANNOT REMOVE ME FROM THE SCHOOL. I <u>AM</u> THE SCHOOL. THE SCHOOL IS <u>ME</u>."**

Jasper staggered backward as the yelling grew louder.

Orson's deep voice boomed like thunder. **"JASPER, YOU ARE FAMILY!"**

Sam didn't want to waste this opportunity. *This is my chance to talk some sense into Orson!* he thought.

"Orson! Listen!" Sam shouted. "It's me, Sam Graves."

"SAM GRAVES . . . YOU HAVE DEFEATED ME TIME AND AGAIN! WHY WOULD I LISTEN TO YOU?"

"Because I am the hall monitor!" Sam yelled. He whipped his sash from his backpack and threw it on.

"Now tell me," Sam continued. "Why do you want to put everyone in danger?"

"SO I CAN LIVE FOREVER!"

"But you're using this school *for evil*!" Sam exclaimed. "I've seen your old science book . . . I know you loved to learn! I know you built this school *for* the students! Think about the students now!"

Orson's voice changed. It sounded more thoughtful. **"I . . . I MUST . . . ALL OF THIS . . . ALL THAT I'VE ACCOMPLISHED . . . IT IS MY LIFE'S WORK."**

Sam felt a change in Orson. The rage and anger faded away. He felt something *good* inside Orson.

But then, suddenly, Orson roared. **"NO! YOU ARE MY ENEMY! THE HALL MONITOR HAS ALWAYS BEEN MY ENEMY!"**

With that, the machine leapt into the air — like an invisible hand had plucked it from the ground. The machine *ripped itself* apart. Sparks showered the floor.

"Get down!" Lucy shouted. She and Antonio dove beneath a workbench.

But Jasper didn't move. *He's frozen with fear!* Sam realized.

Sam grabbed hold of Jasper, dragging him to safety.

And just in time —
SMASH!!!

The machine crashed back down. Bits of broken metal skittered across the floor.

Sam gulped. *We made contact with Orson Eerie. We were <u>so close</u>. But just like that, the machine has been destroyed.*

Jasper's face was paper white. He raced for the door. "It's hopeless!" he cried.

KA-KA-KRACK!

The floor split apart at Jasper's feet. Tiles formed a wave, lifting him up! Jasper reached for the door, but he was hurled into a supply shelf. The shelf toppled over — showering him with crayons, brushes, and glue.

The friends rushed toward Jasper, but the tiles beneath *their* feet began swirling. The floor turned into a giant whirlpool, whipping them around the room.

Finally, they were hurled into a corner, far away from Jasper.

"I'm sorry I failed . . ." Sam told his friends. "I couldn't convince Orson Eerie to stop. He'll *never* stop. *Orson Eerie is evil.*"

Smashed machinery was strewn across the floor. The machine had been ripped, wrecked, and shattered.

But the battle wasn't over . . .

The floor tiles rose up, joining with the broken machine, transforming —

Sam gasped.

The floor and the debris were taking the shape of a person.

The person.

Him.

Orson Eerie.

ENORMOUS ORSON

14

Orson Eerie became taller and larger until he filled the room.

Sam could not believe his eyes.

Orson turned and scooped up his great-great-grandson, Jasper. The substitute teacher dangled from Orson's giant monster hand.

Orson's massive machine neck craned to look at Jasper.

And that's when Sam spotted it: the red lever that turned the machine on and off! *If I could reach that lever,* Sam thought, *maybe I could stop this monster!*

"Lucy! Antonio!" Sam said as he scrambled to his feet. "Orson is going to drop Jasper! Can you guys find a way to break his fall?"

Lucy took a step forward. "We'll figure something out."

"Sam, what are you going to do?" Antonio asked.

But Sam didn't respond — he was already racing across the room. He gripped the leg of this monstrous Orson Eerie and pulled himself upward.

Just like climbing a tree, Sam told himself.

Orson shook Jasper in his giant hand.

Sam climbed higher and higher. His arms were sore, and sweat dripped down his face. Soon he grasped the metal tube that was now Orson's torso. He kept climbing.

Down below, Antonio and Lucy grabbed a huge box labeled RUBBER ERASERS. They turned the box over, dumping out thousands of pink erasers. Then they both ran around, spreading them all over the floor.

Pulling himself up, Sam came to Orson's shoulder. The lever jutted out from the back of Orson's neck.

Orson's massive face craned to the side. His eyes focused on Sam's shiny, orange hall monitor sash.

Sam ignored Orson's terrifying gaze and reached for the lever.

Sam's fingers grazed the cool metal.

He was *so* close. All he had to do was pull it, but —

Orson plucked Sam from his shoulder!

He held Sam in one hand and Jasper Eerie in the other.

Then, from twenty feet high, he dropped them . . .

SLIPPING UP

15

Sam and Jasper bounced off the eraser-covered floor. The soft rubber broke their fall — just like a gym mat.

Lucy and Antonio ran over to them.

"Thank you!" Jasper exclaimed.

"Nice save!" Sam said, sitting up. "But we're not in the clear yet!"

The gigantic Orson Eerie was stomping toward them. He was so gigantic that every movement seemed to happen in slow motion.

"We have to take him down!" Sam yelled.

"That's it!" Lucy exclaimed. "*Down!* All the way down!"

Glancing around, Lucy spotted a huge can of oil paint. "Guys, oil is slippery!" she continued. "Help me open these paint cans!"

Antonio yanked the lid off a can.

"Bu— bu— but Orson can see what you're doing," Jasper said.

"You guys handle the paint!" said Sam. "I'll keep Orson busy!"

Sam stepped forward. He held the hall monitor sash up high. Orson's strange metal eyes focused on the shiny sash.

"Come on, you crazy old mad scientist!" Sam shouted.

"ARGHHHH!" Orson howled and stomped closer.

Out of the corner of Sam's eye, he saw Antonio and Lucy opening the paint cans.

KA-SPLOOSH!

They splashed the paint across the floor. Green and orange and blue and red splattered the ground.

Orson's hand reached for Sam. Sam stepped backward, leading Orson forward. And just as Orson took his next step —

AARGHHH! Orson howled as his feet went out from under him.

Jasper grabbed Sam, yanking him away just as —

KA-BOOM!

Orson Eerie's strange and jumbled body smashed to the floor. It was the loudest sound Sam had ever heard. It felt like an earthquake as giant Orson cracked apart and exploded outward.

CLOSER THAN EVER

The art room door flew open. Principal Winik burst inside, followed by Mr. Nekobi.

"What was that noise?" Principal Winik asked. He eyed the paint dripping from the walls and the machine parts scattered across

Sam didn't know what to say. Thankfully, Mr. Nekobi did. "The floor-cleaning machine was very old. We will get this mess cleaned up. Don't worry."

"Fine," Principal Winik said.

Sam flashed a relieved smile at Lucy and Antonio.

What would we do without Mr. Nekobi? Sam thought.

Principal Winik turned to Jasper Eerie. Jasper's face was colorless. "You don't look well," Principal Winik said. "I can't have *you* missing school, too! Let's go see the school nurse."

Principal Winik hurried into the hall.

At the doorway, Jasper stopped. He turned to Sam, Lucy, and Antonio.

"I'm afraid I'm going to disappoint your principal — and you," Jasper said. "I won't be back tomorrow. I won't be back here ever again . . ."

"But you have to help us!" Sam exclaimed.

"I will try," Jasper replied. "I will keep studying my great-great-grandfather's papers. And you are welcome to explore my house anytime. Who knows what secrets it holds . . . But I can't return here. You three are far braver than I am."

Antonio grinned. "Aww, shucks. Us?" he said with a laugh.

Lucy laughed, too. "*You're* the one who has to sleep in that creepy house, Mr. Eerie. You're plenty brave."

He nodded gently and gave Sam one final look.

Then he was gone.

"Now let's get this room cleaned up," Mr. Nekobi said, handing out mops. "Tomorrow is another day."

"But we were so close . . ." Sam said.

Antonio slapped Sam on the back. "And that's a good thing!"

"We may not have defeated Orson Eerie this time," Lucy said. "But now we've talked to him. We know what he's thinking, and we know how he was created. And you know what that means?"

Sam smiled at his friends. "It means we're closer to destroying him," he said. "You're right. We can do it. We *will* do it. Together."

Shhhh!

This news is top secret:

Jack Chabert is a pen name for Max Brallier. (Max uses a made-up name instead of his real name so Orson Eerie won't come after him, too!)

Max was once a hall monitor at Joshua Eaton Elementary School in Reading, MA. But today, Max lives in a weird, old apartment building in New York City. His days are spent writing, playing video games, and reading comic books. And at night, he walks the halls, always prepared for the moment when his building will come alive.

Max is the author of more than twenty books for children, including the middle-grade series The Last Kids on Earth and Galactic Hot Dogs.

Sam Ricks went to a haunted elementary school, but he never got to be the hall monitor. As far as Sam knows, the school never tried to eat him. Sam graduated from The University of Baltimore with a master's degree in design. During the day, he illustrates from the comfort of his non-carnivorous home. And at night, he reads strange tales to his four children.

HOW MUCH DO YOU KNOW ABOUT

Eerie Elementary

Sam BATTLES the Machine?

Why are Sam, Lucy, and Antonio afraid of their substitute teacher at first?

What does Jasper Eerie plan to do with the strange machine?

Look back at pages 67–68. What does Sam say that seems to surprise Orson Eerie? Why does the tone of Orson's voice change?

How does the machine change from the beginning of the story to the end of the story?

What secrets do **you** think are hiding in Orson's house? Use words and pictures to show what you think might be there!